The Ugly Duckling

and other stories

Miles KeLLY

First published in 2011 by Miles Kelly Publishing Ltd
Harding's Barn, Bardfield End Green, Thaxted, Essex, CM6 3PX, UK

2 4 6 8 10 9 7 5 3 1

Publishing Director Belinda Gallagher

Creative Director Jo Cowan

Editor Amanda Askew

Senior Designer Joe Jones

Designer Kayleigh Allen

Production Manager Elizabeth Collins

Reprographics Anthony Cambray, Stephan Davis, Jennifer Hunt

ISBN 978-1-84810-437-2

Printed in China

British Library Cataloguing-in-Publication Data
A catalogue record for this book is available from the British Library

ACKNOWLEDGEMENTS
Artworks are from the Miles Kelly Artwork Bank

Made with paper from a sustainable forest

www.mileskelly.net
info@mileskelly.net

www.factsforprojects.com

Self-publish your
children's book

buddingpress.co.uk

Contents

The Cat and the Mouse

By the Brothers Grimm

Now this is the tale of a wily cat and a foolish mouse. The mouse lived in a bare mouse hole under the pulpit in the church. The cat lived on an old cushion in the vestry. They had met on several occasions, the mouse usually whisking herself away very fast to the safety of her hole. She did not like the look of the cat's claws.

One day, the cat called on the mouse at home.

"Miss mouse," a purry voice said, "why don't you

and I set up home together? We could live in the bell tower and look after each other. We could share our food, too."

The mouse thought about this carefully. She had never been fond of cats ever since her great grandfather had been supper for the farm tom cat one cold, frosty night. But she could see that there would be benefits. The cat had a nice smile on his face. So she agreed.

They put their savings together and bought a pot full of fat for the winter. The cat said he would hide it away safely under the altar where no one ever went, and so it was done. They both promised not to touch it until the weather became really bad.

The mouse went about her business, quite happy in her new home, although she found the stairs wearisome. But the cat could not stop thinking about the pot of fat. So he thought up a plan.

"My cousin has just had a kitten," he told the mouse. "And she wants me to be godcat. I should like to go to the christening, would you mind?"

"Not at all, Mister cat," said the mouse. "I have plenty to do today."

But the wicked Cat went straight to the pot of fat and ate the top off. Then he went to sleep for the rest of the day. When it was evening, he stretched and strolled back up to the bell tower.

"Did you have a nice time?" asked the mouse

"Oh yes, very nice," said the not-very-nice cat.

"And what is the kitten called?"

"Topoff," replied the cat.

"Topoff?" asked the mouse. "That is a very strange name. Still I suppose cats have different family names," and she went on with her work.

All was quiet for a few days but then the cat had great longings for the pot of fat again so he went to the mouse.

"I find I have another new godkitten. Would you mind if I went to the christening?" said the cat, his green eyes half closed.

"Another godkitten?" said the mouse. "My, my you do have a big family."

And the beastly cat slunk off and ate up half the pot of fat. When he sauntered back up the stairs that night the mouse was waiting.

"Well, how did it all go?" she said. "What is this kitten to be called?"

"Halfempty," replied the cat.

"Halfempty?" said the mouse. "I have never heard such a thing before."

But the cat was asleep, a smile twitching his whiskers.

Well, as you can imagine, it was not long before that greedy cat wanted some fat again.

"Miss mouse, just imagine! I have yet another godkitten. I should really go to this christening too," he said.

Miss mouse thought it all very strange but she was a kindly creature so she waved the cat off to yet another christening. The cat, of course, just scuttled downstairs, slid under the altar and licked the pot of fat quite clean. He came back very late that night.

"What strange name did your family give this new kitten?" asked the mouse crossly. She had a headache from all the noise in the tower when the bells rang.

"Allgone," said the cat.

"Topoff, Halfempty and now Allgone!" the mouse said in disbelief. "Well, I am glad I am not a member of your family. I couldn't be doing with such weird names," and she went to sleep with her paws over her ears. There were no more christenings. The weather became colder, and the mouse began to think of the pot of fat hidden under the altar.

"Mister cat," she said one frosty morning, "I think it is time we collected our pot of fat. I am looking forward to a lick."

'We'll see about that', thought the cat, but he padded downstairs behind the mouse. She reached under the altar and brought out the pot, but of course when she looked in, it was all empty.

"What a foolish mouse I have been!" she cried. "Now I see what a wicked cat you have been. Topoff, Halfempty and Allgone indeed!"

"Such is the way of cats," said the cat, and he grabbed at her with his paw. But she was too quick for him, and dived back into her dear little mouse hole.

Never ever again did she trust cats.

The Ugly Duckling

By Hans Christian Andersen

The mother duck was waiting for her eggs to hatch. Slowly the first shell cracked. A tiny bill and a little yellow wing appeared. Then with a rush, a bedraggled yellow duckling fell out. He stretched his wings and began to clean his feathers. Soon he stood beside his mother, watching as his sisters and brothers all pushed their way out of their shells.

Only one shell was left. It was the largest, and the mother duck wondered why it was taking longer than the others. She wanted to take her babies down to the river for their first swimming lesson. There was a loud crack, and there lay the biggest, ugliest duckling she had ever seen. He wasn't even yellow – his feathers were brown and grey.

"Oh dear," said the mother duck.

She led the family down to the river, the ugly duckling trailing along behind the others. They all splashed into the water, and were soon swimming gracefully – all except the ugly duckling who looked large and ungainly even on the water.

"Oh dear," said the mother duck.

The whole family set off for the farmyard where they were greeted with hoots and moos and barks and snorts from all the other animals.

"Whatever is that?" said the rooster, pointing rudely at the ugly duckling. All the other ducklings huddled round their mother and tried to pretend the ugly duckling was not with them.

"Oh dear," said the mother duck.

The ugly duckling felt very sad and lonely. No one seemed to like him, so he ran away from the farmyard and hid in some dark reeds by the river. Some hunters came by with their loud noisy guns and big fierce dogs.

The ugly duckling paddled deeper into the reeds, trembling with fear. Only later in the day, as it was growing dark, did he stir from his hiding place.

All summer he wandered over fields and down rivers. Everywhere he went people laughed and jeered at him, and other ducks just hissed at him or tried to bite his tail. As well as being ugly, the duckling was very lonely and unhappy. Soon winter came and the rivers began to freeze over. One day the duckling found himself trapped in the ice. He tucked his head under his wing, and decided that his short life must have come to an end.

He was still there early the next morning when a farmer came by on his way to feed the cows in the fields. The farmer broke the ice with his shoe, wrapped the ugly duckling in his jacket and carried him home to his children. They put the poor frozen ugly duckling in a box by the fire, and as he thawed out they fed him and stroked his feathers. And there the ugly duckling stayed through the winter, growing bigger all the time.

Now the farmer's wife had never had much time for the ugly duckling. He was always getting under her feet in the kitchen, and he was so clumsy that he kept knocking things over. He spilt the milk in the bucket from the cow. He put his great feet in the freshly churned butter. He was just a nuisance, and one day the farmer's wife had enough. So, in a rage, she chased him out of her kitchen, out of the farmyard and through the gate down the lane.

It was a perfect spring day. The apple trees were covered in blossom and the air was filled with the sound of birdsong. The ugly duckling wandered down to the river, and there he saw three magnificent white swans. They were so beautiful and graceful as they glided towards the bank where he stood. He waited for them to hiss at him and beat the water with their wings to frighten him away, but they didn't do any such thing. Instead they called him to come and join them. At first he thought it was a joke, but they asked him again.

He bent down to get into the water, and there looking back at him was his own reflection. But where was the ugly duckling? All he could see was another great and magnificent swan. He was a swan! Not an ugly duckling, but a swan. He lifted his long elegant neck, and called in sheer delight, "I am a swan! I am a SWAN!" and he sailed gracefully over the water to join his real family.

The Three Billy Goats Gruff

A European folk tale

In a mountain valley beside a rushing river, there lived three billy goats. One was very small, one was middle-sized and one was huge, and they were called the Three Billy Goats Gruff. Every day they would eat the lush green grass by the river, and they were very content.

One day, however, the Three Billy Goats Gruff decided they would like to cross the river and see if the grass was any greener on the other side. The grass was actually no greener, nor was it any tastier, but they all felt they would like a change. First they had to find a way to cross the rushing river. They trotted a good way upstream before they found a little wooden bridge. After a supper of lush green grass, they decided to wait until next morning before crossing the wooden bridge, so they settled down for the night.

The Three Billy Goats Gruff

Now, what the Three Billy Goats Gruff did not know was that under the little wooden bridge there lived a very mean and grumpy troll. He could smell the Three Billy Goats Gruff, and he thought they smelled good to eat. So the next morning when the Three Billy Goats Gruff had eaten a breakfast of lush green grass, the troll was hiding under the little wooden bridge, waiting for his chance to have breakfast too.

"That little wooden bridge does not look too strong," said the very small Billy Goat Gruff. "I will go across first to see if it is safe," and he trotted across the little wooden bridge. But when he was only halfway across, the mean and grumpy troll leapt out of his hiding place.

"Who is that trit-trotting across my bridge?" he roared. "I am going to eat you up!"

But the very small Billy Goat Gruff wasn't ready

to be eaten up just yet, so he bravely said to the mean and grumpy troll, "You don't want to eat a skinny, bony thing like me. Just wait till my brother comes across, he is much bigger." And with a skip and a hop, the very small Billy Goat Gruff ran across the bridge to the lush green grass on the other side.

The middle-sized Billy Goat Gruff started to cross the little wooden bridge, but when he was only halfway across, the mean and grumpy troll roared at him, "Who is that trit-trotting across my bridge? I am going to eat you up!"

But the middle-sized Billy Goat Gruff wasn't ready to be eaten up just yet either, so he bravely said to the mean and grumpy troll, "You don't want to eat a skinny, bony thing like me. Wait till my brother comes across, he is even bigger." And with a skip and a hop, the middle-sized Billy Goat Gruff ran across the bridge to the lush green grass on the other side.

Now, the huge Billy Goat Gruff had been watching all the time. He smiled to himself and stepped onto the little wooden bridge. By this time the troll was very hungry , and he was even meaner and grumpier when he was hungry. He didn't bother to hide, but stood in the middle of the bridge looking at the huge

Billy Goat Gruff who came trotting up to him.

"Who is that trit-trotting across my bridge?" he roared. "I am going to eat you up!"

"Oh no, you won't!" said the huge Billy Goat Gruff, and he lowered his head and with his huge horns he biffed the mean and grumpy troll into the rushing river. The water carried him far away down the river, and he was never seen again. The Three Billy Goats Gruff lived happily for many more years eating the lush green grass, and they were able to cross the river whenever they wanted!

The Seven Little Kids

By the Brothers Grimm

There was once a mother goat who had seven little kids. One day she had to go into the wood to fetch food for them, so she called them to her.

"Dear children," said she, "While I am gone, watch out for the wolf. If he gets in he will eat you up. He often disguises himself, but he may always be known by his hoarse voice and black paws."

"Mother," said the kids, "you need not be afraid, we will take care of ourselves."

Soon the kids heard knocking at the door, and a voice cried, "Open the door children, your mother has returned, and brought each of you something."

But they knew it was the wolf by the hoarse voice.

"We will not open the door," they cried, "you are not our mother. She has a delicate and sweet voice, and your voice is hoarse – you must be the wolf!"

The wolf went to a shop and bought a big lump of chalk, and ate it up to make his voice soft. Then he came back, knocked at the door and cried, "Open the door children, your mother has returned, and brought each of you something."

But the wolf had put his black paws up against the window, and the kids cried out, "We will not open the door, our mother has no black paws – you must be the wolf!"

The wolf ran to a baker. "Baker," said he, "I have hurt my feet, pray spread some dough over them."

When the baker had done so, the wolf ran to the miller and said, "Cover my paws with white flour." The miller refused, thinking the wolf must wish to harm to someone.

"If you don't," cried the wolf, "I'll eat you up!"

And the miller was afraid and did as he was told.

Now the wolf arrived at the door again and knocked. "Open children!" cried he, "Your mother has returned, and brought each of you something."

"Show us your paws," said the kids.

The wolf put his paws up to the window, and when the kids saw that they were white they opened the door.

When the door opened and he entered they saw it was the wolf. The kids tried to hide. One ran under the table, the second got into bed, the third into the oven, the fourth in the kitchen, the fifth in the cupboard, the sixth under the sink and the seventh in the clock-case.

But the wolf found them, and swallowed them all – all but the youngest, hidden in the clock-case. Having eaten his fill, the wolf strolled into the meadow, lay himself down under a tree, and fell asleep.

When the mother goat returned, a horrible sight met her. The door was open, table and chairs were thrown about, and dishes were broken. Her children were nowhere to be seen. She called to them but none answered, until she came to the youngest.

"Here I am, mother," a little voice cried, "Here, in the clock-case."

She helped him out and heard how the wolf had come, and eaten all the rest. How she cried for the loss of her dear children! At last she left her house, the youngest kid with her. When they came to the meadow they saw the wolf lying under a tree, snoring. The mother goat looked at him carefully on all sides and she noticed how something inside him was moving and struggling.

'Dear me!' thought she, 'can it be that my poor children are still alive?' And she sent the little kid back to the house for a pair of shears, a needle and some thread. Then she cut the wolf open – no sooner had she made one snip than out came the head of one of the kids. One after another the six little kids all jumped out alive and well, for in his greediness the rogue had swallowed them whole.

"Now fetch some hard stones," said the mother, "and we will fill his body with them while he sleeps."

They put the stones inside him, and the mother sewed him up quickly so that he was none the wiser.

When the wolf awoke, the stones inside him made him very thirsty. As he was going to the brook to drink, they rattled against each other. He cried out,

"What is this I feel inside me

Knocking hard against my bones?

How should such a thing betide me!

They were kids, and now they're stones."

He came to the brook and stooped to drink, but the heavy stones weighed him down, and he fell into the water and was drowned.

The little kids saw him fall. "The wolf is dead!" they cried, and they danced all about the place.

The Sagacious Monkey and the Boar

By Yei Theodora Ozaki

Long ago, in the province of Shinshin in Japan, there lived a travelling monkey man. He earned money by taking round a monkey and showing off its tricks. One day he came home very cross and told his wife to send for the butcher in the morning.

His wife was bewildered and asked her husband, "Why do you wish me to send for the butcher?"

"It's no use taking that monkey round any longer, he's old and he forgets his tricks. I beat him with my stick, but he won't dance properly. I must now sell him to the butcher and make what money out of him I can. There is nothing else to be done."

The woman felt sorry for the poor animal, and pleaded for her husband to spare the monkey, but her pleading was in vain, the man was determined.

Now the monkey was in the next room and he had overheard every word. He understood that he was to be killed, and he said to himself, "Barbarous, indeed, is my master! Here I have served him faithfully for years, and instead of allowing me to end my days comfortably, he is going to let me be cut up by the butcher, and my poor body is to be roasted and stewed and eaten? What am I to do? Ah! A thought has struck me! There is a wild boar living in the forest nearby. I have often heard tell of his wisdom. Perhaps if I tell him the strait I am in he will give me his counsel. I will go and try."

The monkey slipped out of the house and ran to find the boar. The boar was at home, and the monkey told his tale of woe. "Mr Boar, I have heard of your wisdom. I am in great trouble. I have grown old in the service of my master, and because I now cannot dance he intends to sell me to the butcher. What do you advise? I know how clever you are!"

The boar thought for a while and then said, "Has your master a baby?"

"Oh, yes," said the monkey, "he has a baby son."

"Does it lie by the door in the morning? Well, I will come round early, seize the baby and run off with it."

"What then?" said the monkey.

"You must run after me and rescue the child and take it home safely to its parents. When the butcher comes they won't have the heart to sell you."

The monkey thanked the boar and went home.

In the morning he was the first up, waiting

anxiously for what was to happen. It seemed to him a very long time before his master's wife began to move about and open the shutters.

Luckily, everything happened as the boar had planned. The mother placed her child near the porch as usual while she got the breakfast ready.

The child was crooning happily in the morning sunlight, dabbing on the mats at the play of light

and shadow. Suddenly there was
a noise in the porch and a loud cry from
the child. The mother called her husband
from the inner room where he was still
sleeping soundly, and they both ran to the
porch door just in time to see the boar
disappearing with their child. Then they
saw the monkey running after the thief
as hard as his legs would carry him.

Both the man and wife were moved to admiration at the plucky conduct of the sagacious monkey, and their gratitude knew no bounds when the faithful monkey brought the child safely back to their arms.

"There!" said the wife. "This is the animal you want to kill — if the monkey hadn't been here we should have lost our child forever."

"You are right, wife," said the man as he carried the child into the house. "You may send the butcher back when he comes, and now give us all a good breakfast and the monkey too."

When the butcher arrived he was sent away with an order for some boar's meat for the evening dinner, and the monkey was petted and lived the rest of his days in peace, nor did his master ever strike him again.

How the Camel got his Hump

By Rudyard Kipling

In the beginning of years, when the world was new-and-all, and the animals were beginning to work for man, there was a camel. He lived in the middle of a desert because he did not want to work. He ate sticks, thorns and tamarisks, milkweed and prickles. He was most idle, and when anybody spoke to him he said "Humph!"

Presently the horse came to him on Monday morning, with a saddle on his back and a bit in his mouth, and said, "Camel, come and trot like the rest of us."

"Humph!" said the camel, and the horse went away and told the man.

Presently the dog came to him with a stick in his mouth, and said, "Camel, come and fetch and carry like the rest of us."

"Humph!" said the camel and the dog went away to tell the man.

Presently the ox came to him, with the yoke on his neck and said, "Camel, come and plough like the rest of us."

"Humph!" said the camel, and the ox went away and told the man.

At the end of the day the man called the horse

and the dog and the ox together, and said, "Three, I'm sorry for you, but that thing in the desert can't work. You must work double to make up for it."

That made the Three angry (with the world so new-and-all), and they held a palaver and a pow-wow on the edge of the desert, and the camel came and laughed at them. Then he said "Humph!" and went away again.

Presently there came along the djinn in charge of All Deserts, and he stopped to palaver and pow-pow with the Three.

"Djinn of All Deserts," said the horse, "is it right to be idle, with the world so new-and-all?"

"Certainly not," said the djinn.

"Well," said the horse, "there's a thing in the middle of your desert with a long neck and long legs, and he hasn't done a stroke of work since Monday morning. He won't trot."

"Whew!" said the djinn, whistling, "that's my camel! What does he say about it?"

"He says Humph!" said the dog, "And he won't fetch and carry."

"Does he say anything else?"

"Only Humph! And he won't plough," said the ox.

"Very good," said the djinn. "I'll humph him if you will kindly wait a minute."

The djinn found the camel looking at his own reflection in a pool of water.

"My long and bubbling friend," said the djinn, "what's this I hear of you doing no work, with the world so new-and-all?"

"Humph!" said the camel.

The djinn sat down, with his chin in his hand, and began to think a great magic. "You've given the Three extra work ever since Monday morning, all on account of your idleness," said the djinn.

"Humph!" said the camel.

"I shouldn't say that again if I were you," said the djinn, "You might say it once too often. Bubbles, I want you to work."

And the camel said "Humph!" again, but no sooner had he said it than he saw his back, that he was so proud of, puffing up into a great big humph.

"Do you see that?" said the djinn. "That's your very own humph that you've brought upon your very own self by not working. Today is Thursday, and you've done no work since Monday, when the work began. Now you are going to work."

"How can I," said the camel, "with this humph on my back?"

"That's made on purpose," said the djinn, "all because you missed those three days. You will be able to work now for three days without eating, because you can live on your humph, and don't you ever say I never did anything for you. Come out of the desert and go to the Three, and behave."

And the camel humphed himself, humph and all, and went away to join the Three. And from that day to this the camel always wears a humph (we call it 'hump' now, not to hurt his feelings) but he has never yet caught up with the three days that he missed at the beginning of the world, and he has never yet learned how to behave.